Nimrit
kaur
Sohal

First published by Parragon in 2011

Parragon
Queen Street House
4 Queen Street
Bath BA1 1HE, UK

Printed in China

Storybook
Collection

PaRragon

Bath · New York · Singapore · Hong Kong · Cologne · Delhi
Melbourne · Amsterdam · Johannesburg · Auckland · Shenzhen

This book belongs to:

Nimrit Sohal

Contents

Belle and the Castle Puppy

By Barbara Bazaldua

Illustrated by STUDIO IBOIX, Marco Colletti and Elena Naggi

Belle was strolling through the castle garden one chilly spring day, when she heard a whimpering sound. A shivering puppy was huddled by the castle gates.

"Oh, you poor thing!" Belle cried. "Let's get you warmed up and fed!" She cuddled the puppy in her red cloak and hurried to the castle kitchen.

The enchanted objects laughed when he splashed in his bath. The dinner forks combed his fur while he gobbled a bowl of warm stew. Chip and his brothers and sisters giggled when the puppy drank water from them.

"He's so cute! I hope we can keep him!" Chip said.

But one enchanted object didn't join the fun.

The ottoman watched the puppy. He remembered when he had been a real dog. Suddenly, he wanted some attention, too. With a funny little "grrr," he thumped around the kitchen, trying to act like the puppy. But no one noticed.

Just then, the puppy bounded to the door, barking eagerly.

"Do you want to go out to play?" Belle asked, opening the door.

As Belle and the others followed the puppy outside, they didn't see the ottoman slink out and wander off alone. They laughed as Belle threw sticks for the puppy to fetch. Just then, the Beast walked up the path, clutching one of his precious rosebushes. "Someone has dug up my roses!" he exclaimed.

Then the Beast saw the puppy.

"Did that dog dig up my garden? Get rid of him – NOW!"

"I can't leave him in the woods," Belle argued. "He needs a home."

"He's not getting one here!" the Beast roared as he stomped away into the forest. Belle knew that the Beast loved his roses, but what about the puppy?

Just then, the ottoman ran past Belle and the others. His legs were muddy.

"Ottoman dug up the garden!" Belle exclaimed.

"But why?" Lumiere asked.

As Belle watched the ottoman racing after the Beast, she suddenly understood.

"Oh, poor Ottoman," Belle said. "He just wanted some attention, too!"

Suddenly, the
puppy raced after the
ottoman, barking playfully.

Belle tried to call to them, but
the ottoman and puppy disappeared
among the trees.

"They'll get lost!" Belle exclaimed.
"I have to bring them back safely."

"But it's getting dark," Mrs Potts protested.

21

Belle looked at the long shadows creeping through the forest and shivered. Clutching her red cloak tightly, she took a deep breath and started toward the trees.

"Wait!" Lumiere called. "I'll come and light your way."

"Thank you," Belle said as she held Lumiere up high. "I'm glad you're coming."

"Me, too. I think," Lumiere replied. But his flames flickered nervously.

"Puppy! Ottoman!" Belle called as she and Lumiere searched. Something rustled in the bushes. Yellow eyes gleamed at them.

"What is that?" Lumiere whispered.

"I hope it's just squirrels," Belle answered.

"It must be very big squirrels with very big eyes," Lumiere replied.

Belle picked up a large stick. Then she and Lumiere walked on, calling and calling.

Suddenly, they heard ferocious barking and snarling nearby. Belle ran toward the sound and stumbled into a clearing. The ottoman and puppy stood below an enormous tree. Snarling wolves circled them. But the puppy was growling and snapping back.

"He's protecting Ottoman!" Lumiere exclaimed.

"He's too small to stop those wolves for long," Belle answered. "He needs help!"

Quickly, Belle put Lumiere on the ground and lit the stick with his flames. Turning swiftly, Belle ran at the wolves, swinging the blazing stick at them like a flaming sword.

"Get away! Get away!" she shouted.

Snarling angrily, the wolves backed away from the fire. Belle raced between them towards the ottoman and puppy.

But just then Belle tripped on a root. The torch flew from her hands.

"Oh, no!" she gasped.

The torch hit the ground and rolled just out of her reach. The growling wolves crept towards her.

Barking fiercely, the puppy raced to the flaming stick. He snatched one end in his teeth and darted among the wolves. As the wolves backed away, the ottoman ran in front of Belle, yapping for her to follow.

"The puppy's clearing the way!" Lumiere shouted. "Follow Ottoman!"

Suddenly, the Beast crashed into the clearing. The wolves scattered yelping with fear.

The danger had passed. But the puppy's nose and ears were singed and sore.

"He and the ottoman tried to save me!" Belle said.

"They are brave little fellows," the Beast answered.

Cradling the puppy in one arm, and the ottoman in the other, he led Belle to the castle.

When the puppy was cared for, everyone settled by the fireside. Belle watched the Beast stroke the ottoman and feed the puppy biscuits. The gentle smile on his face made her happy.

"May the puppy stay until I can find him a home?" she asked.

The Beast cleared his throat. "His home is here – with us," he answered gruffly. Belle smiled, knowing the Beast loved both of his pets dearly.

The next evening as Belle and the Beast waltzed in the ballroom, the puppy and ottoman kept guard proudly at the door. Both the puppy and the ottoman wore shiny new badges. And on each badge were the words, "Protector of the House."

The End

Tiana and her Loyal Friend

By Natalie Amanda Leece

Illustrated by Studio IBOIX and Walt Sturrock

It was a balmy afternoon in New Orleans. Big Daddy was in the mood for some good food and good times with friends.

"Charlotte honey!" he called out to his daughter. "How about going to Tiana's Palace for supper tonight?"

"Oh, Daddy, that would be wonderful! Just give me a minute to change."

Later, as they drove off,
nobody noticed Stella the hound
asleep in the back of the car!

But Stella didn't mind. In fact, the one thing that woke her up was the smell of Tiana's beignets when they reached the restaurant. Stella loved Tiana's beignets, so the hound followed her nose right into the restaurant's back kitchen.

"Big Daddy! Charlotte!" Princess Tiana warmly welcomed her friends. "Would you like to sit with my Mama?"

"Why, I can't think of anyone better to share my supper with than Eudora," Big Daddy replied.

Meanwhile, Stella smelled nothing but goodness in the kitchen. "Lookee here!" shouted one of the cooks. "We have a visitor! Here you go, puppy – have some of this gumbo. It's a new recipe!"

Stella spent a happy evening in the kitchen getting well fed and petted, while Charlotte and Big Daddy dined to Louis's jazz music and good conversation with their friends.

43

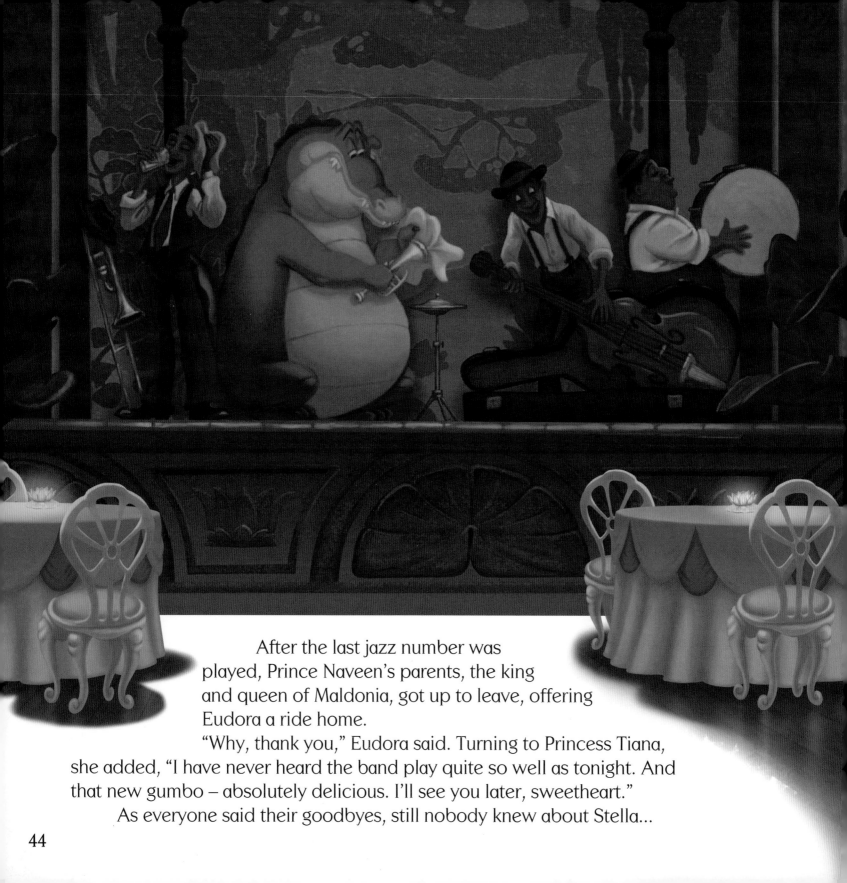

After the last jazz number was
played, Prince Naveen's parents, the king
and queen of Maldonia, got up to leave, offering
Eudora a ride home.

"Why, thank you," Eudora said. Turning to Princess Tiana,
she added, "I have never heard the band play quite so well as tonight. And
that new gumbo – absolutely delicious. I'll see you later, sweetheart."

As everyone said their goodbyes, still nobody knew about Stella...

...not until Louis entered the kitchen for his evening meal with the rest of the band.

"Grrr! Woof!" Stella was terrified of the giant alligator.

"Oh, now hold on, little dog!" Louis spoke to Stella. "I'm not here to eat you. I just wanted a taste of the chefs' new gumbo!"

The kitchen staff backed away.
They just heard growls coming from
the dog and the gator.

Princess Tiana and Prince Naveen also heard the commotion as they re-entered the restaurant after bidding their friends and family good night.

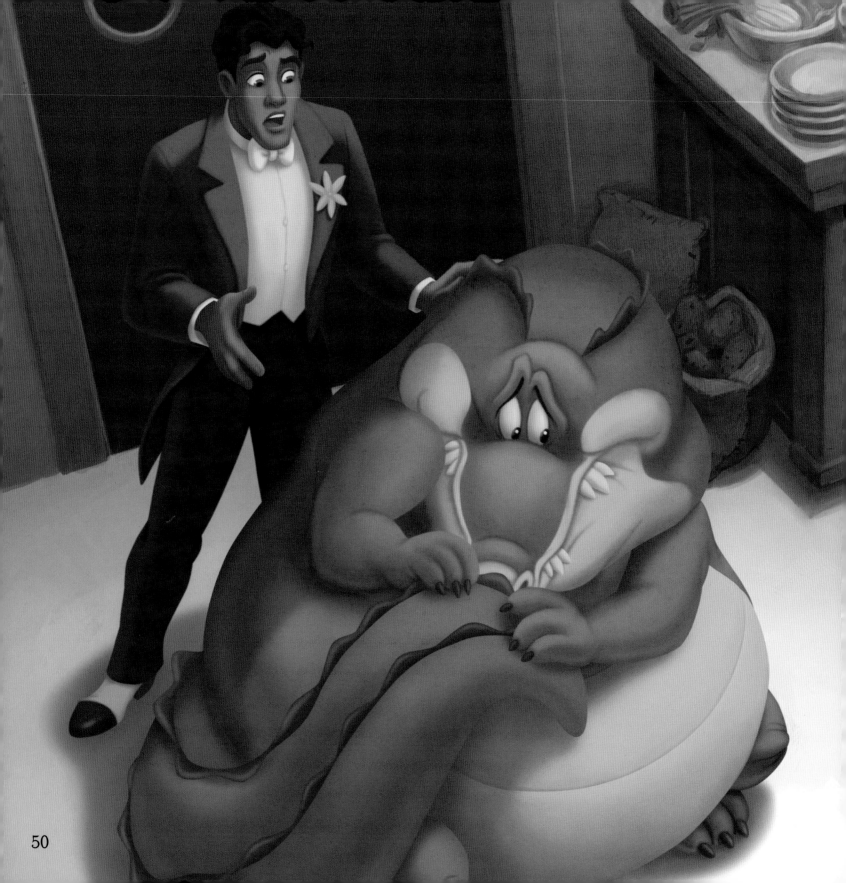

As soon as the prince and princess entered the kitchen, they saw a very frightened Stella plastered against a wall, barking at Louis.

"What is going on with you two?" Princess Tiana said, concerned for Stella.

"Oh, Stella," Princess Tiana said, gently petting the dog. "It's just Louis. He wouldn't hurt anybody."

"That's true!" Naveen cried as he put his arm around Louis. "Louis? He is nothing but a big guy with a bigger heart."

"Go ahead, Stella," Princess Tiana encouraged the dog. "Naveen will hold onto Louis, and you just walk right over to them."

Cautiously, Stella walked toward Louis, with Tiana by her side.

Stella sniffed Louis and then turned back towards the food. Tiana giggled. Naveen giggled. Louis wanted to giggle, but he thought he might scare Stella all over again.

The staff put together a supper made up of that evening's leftovers. Prince Naveen played the ukulele and Tiana made some of her special beignets – just for Stella.

Princess Tiana had to smile. These were truly the good times her father had

imagined having at their restaurant.

Before dawn, the prince and princess dropped Stella off at the LaBouff estate. No one had even noticed she was missing yet!

"Good night, Stella," Princess Tiana said, giving the dog a big hug. "And don't be a stranger. When I stop by, I expect you to come out and get your own beignets."

Stella gave one last woof and went toward the house. She'd had the best night of her life.

The End

Cinderella and the Lost Mice

By E.C. Llopis

Illustrated by: IBOIX and Michael Inman

The stars twinkled in the clear night sky as the prince twirled Cinderella outside to dance.

"Are you cold, my dear?" the Prince asked his princess.

"Just a bit, but—"

Smiling, the Prince reached for a box he had hidden under a bench. Inside was a beautiful winter coat.

"Oh, it's simply lovely!" Cinderella exclaimed. "Thank you!"

The next morning Cinderella showed her coat to Suzy the mouse. "Isn't the Prince kind to me?" she said.

"Nice-a! Nice-a!" Suzy nodded and nuzzled the warm coat.

Cinderella didn't notice that Suzy had just come in from the cold. The tiny mouse was shivering even though the room was warm!

Just then, Gus and Jaq scampered up onto Cinderella's dressing table.
"Cinderelly! Cinderelly!" they chattered.

Cinderella didn't hear them as she rushed off to meet the Prince. She didn't
know that they were cold, too!

63

Soon several more cold and shivering mice entered the room. They sat in front of the fire until their teeth stopped chattering. The poor mice had spent the night in the freezing attic! They hoped Cinderella would let them stay in her warm room. But there was a problem.

"Shoo, shoo!" The cruel housekeeper barged into the room and began chasing the mice! "You're making the whole castle dirty!" she shouted. "I should have the gardener haul you away!" She was the reason that the mice were cold – and scared! They stayed in the attic to hide from her!

The mice scrambled back to the chilly attic, not knowing where else to go. "Cinderelly," Gus sighed. They needed her help!

Suddenly – *WHAM!* – the gardener slammed cages over the mice and scooped them up!

"Now take them outside!" shrieked the housekeeper. "Take them far enough away that they never return!"

Of course, Cinderella had no idea what had happened as she and the Prince strolled along the castle grounds.

"Let's go to the stables!" Cinderella said suddenly. "We can say hello to the horses."

"And maybe take a ride?" the Prince asked hopefully.

"Lovely idea!" Cinderella replied.

Soon Cinderella and the Prince were riding through the countryside near the castle. They saw the gardener doing something in one of the fields.

"Hello!" shouted the Prince. "It's too cold to be working outside!"

But the gardener didn't seem to hear the Prince.

When the Prince and princess returned to the stables, the Prince asked, "Do you think the gardener was acting oddly?"

"Perhaps he was distracted," Cinderella replied thoughtfully. "It must be hard to do much gardening when the ground is frozen."

73

But the gardener was not distracted about gardening. He was worried about the mice! He knew that they would freeze in the fields.

"All right." he said to his helpers. "Now don't mention this to the housekeeper, but I want to bring these poor mice to the stables."

So they took the grateful mice to their new home and even fed them.

The mice nestled together in the barn, but as night approached, they just got colder. Finally the horses allowed them to snuggle up in their manes to keep warm.

"Thassa nice-a," Gus said sleepily.

Meanwhile, Cinderella was beginning to worry. Where were her little friends?

"Jaq and Gus!" she thought suddenly. "They wanted to talk to me this morning, but I left in a rush to see the Prince. I wonder if they needed to tell me something."

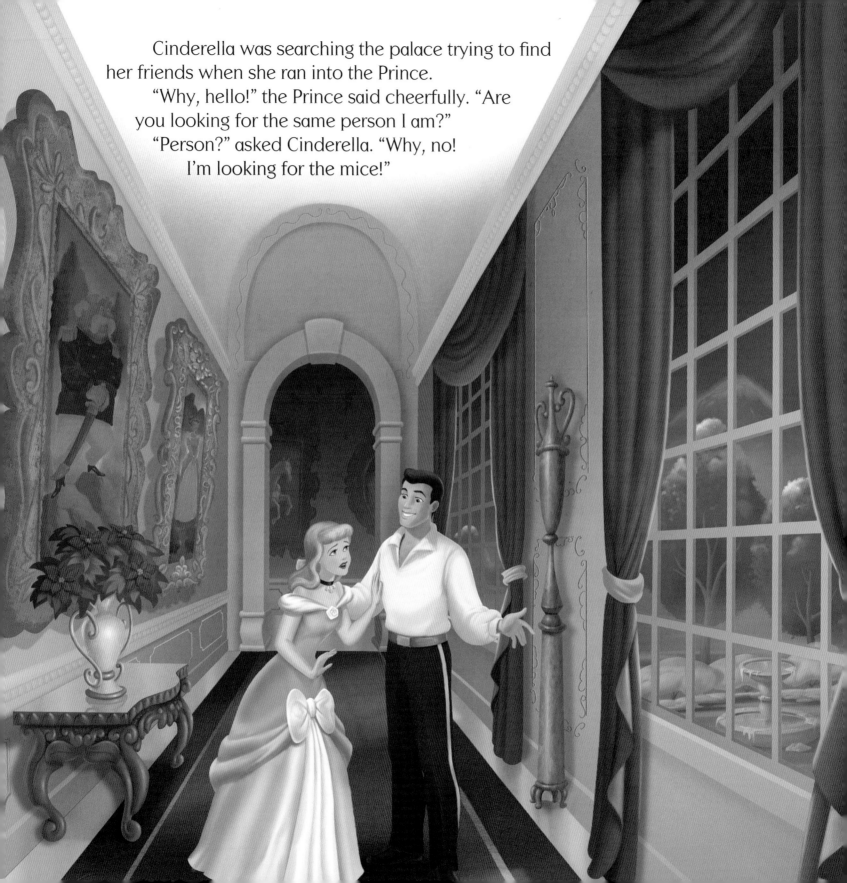

Cinderella was searching the palace trying to find her friends when she ran into the Prince.

"Why, hello!" the Prince said cheerfully. "Are you looking for the same person I am?"

"Person?" asked Cinderella. "Why, no! I'm looking for the mice!"

"Ah," said the Prince. "And I am looking for the housekeeper who apparently threw them out of the castle today. She said they were dirty!"

"Dirty! Oh, no!" Cinderella cried. "They're not dirty. And besides, they'll freeze outside!"

"Don't worry, my dear. The mice have found a new friend." The Prince then told Cinderella about the gardener and what he had done.

Together, Cinderella and the Prince went to the stables, where they found and thanked the gardener. Then Cinderella awakened the mice who were snuggled comfortably in the horses' manes.

"Cinderelly! Cinderelly!" the mice shouted happily.

A few nights later, there was a grand ball – with the gardener as the guest of honour. The cruel housekeeper now peeled potatoes in the kitchen. She would not be bothering the mice again. Meanwhile, the mice celebrated with a banquet of their own. And as for the horses, they got extra apples all-around!

The End

Ariel's Dolphin Adventure

By Lyra Spenser
Illustrated by IBOIX and Andrea Cagol

Oh, Eric! This is wonderful!" Ariel said excitedly as she twirled around the ballroom with her prince. "I can dance with you and see the ocean!"

"Do you miss your sea friends?" he asked.

"Sometimes," Ariel replied a bit sadly. "But I love being with you."

Bright and early the next morning, Prince Eric found Ariel walking along the beach. He knew that she was hoping to see Flounder and Sebastian, as well as her other friends. Sadly, they were nowhere in sight.

Eric caught up with his princess and hugged her as he watched the white-capped waves crashing hard against the shoreline.

"It's rough out there today. If I were a fish, I think I might be too scared to come close to shore," Eric said gently. "Don't worry, Ariel. We'll figure out a way to bring together land and sea. You deserve the best of both worlds."

Later that day, Eric
and Ariel went for a walk.
    "I was thinking about what you
said earlier," Ariel said. "I want to show you
something." She led him straight to a quiet, beautiful
        little lagoon.
        Eric grinned. "I almost kissed you for the first
            time here."
                "Eric, do you think my friends would
                feel safer visiting me here?"
                Eric rubbed his chin. "Hmmm. Maybe."

A few weeks later, Eric found Ariel walking along the beach again.

"Come with me," he said. "I have a surprise for you."

He took her right to the lagoon. It now had a big wall to keep out dangerous sea creatures like sharks, but it also had a gate so that Ariel's friends could enter the lagoon. In fact, Flounder, Scuttle and Sebastian were there to greet her!

"Oh, Eric!" Ariel gasped. "I love it!"

Ariel was so
excited that she waded into the water.
Then she stopped, seeing something
else in the lagoon. "Look!" she exclaimed. As they watched, a baby dolphin leaped out
of the water! "He's just a baby. I wonder where his mother is."

Flounder swam across the lagoon, but the baby dolphin raced away.

"Poor little guy," Flounder said. "He seems scared of me."

"We should find his mother right away!" Ariel said as she gently coaxed the baby to swim over to her.

"I bet she's on the other side of that wall. Don't worry, Ariel!" Flounder said. "We'll find her!"

But Sebastian and Flounder couldn't find the dolphin's mother. "Oh, Ariel! This is terrible," Sebastian said a few days later. "We have looked everywhere under the sea, but cannot find the baby's mother. King Triton will be so angry!"

Ariel was watching the little dolphin swim slowly around the lagoon. Heartbroken, she knew that the confused baby was looking for his mother.

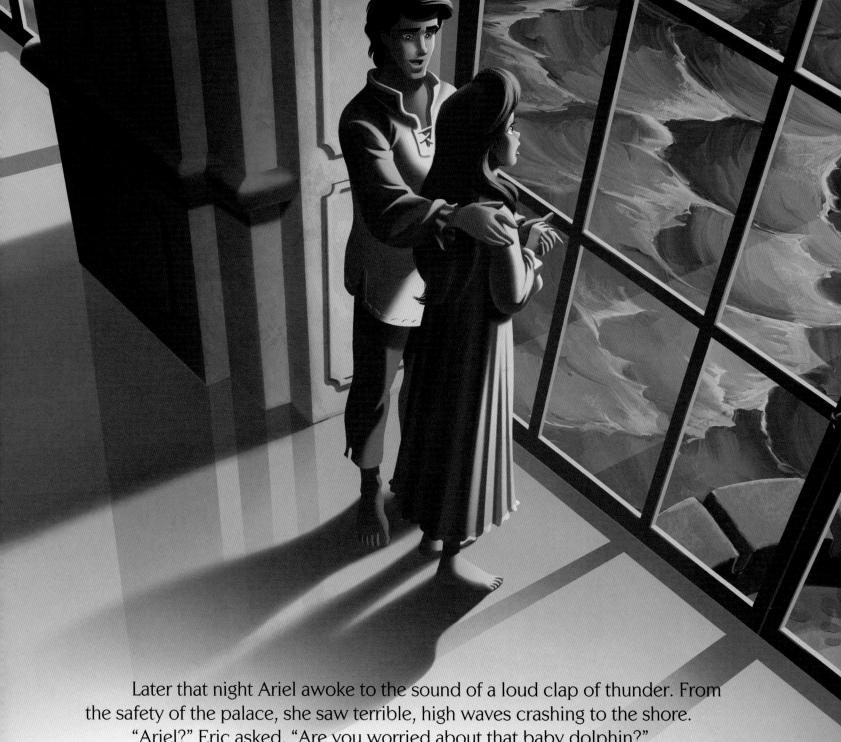

Later that night Ariel awoke to the sound of a loud clap of thunder. From
the safety of the palace, she saw terrible, high waves crashing to the shore.

"Ariel?" Eric asked. "Are you worried about that baby dolphin?"

"Oh, Eric, I am. He must be terrified," she shuddered in reply. "We need
to go to him. And, Eric, I need to ask my father for help."

Eric felt terrible. He now understood that he had made a bad decision by closing in the lagoon. He followed Ariel into the stormy night, ready to help in any way he could.

When they arrived at the lagoon, Flounder was trying to calm the frightened baby dolphin.

"Go to the baby dolphin, Eric," Ariel said gently. "He feels safe with you."

Ariel looked into her prince's eyes, letting him know that she trusted him with her sea friends.

99

Ariel climbed carefully out onto the wall of the lagoon and called to all the sea creatures.

"Help me, please!" she cried out. "I am Ariel, princess of the seas. I need my father, King Triton. Please help!"

Below the surface, sea creatures raced to find King Triton.

Eric tried to keep the baby dolphin safe from the crashing waves. Holding him, Eric led him to the calmer waters near some rocks. Suddenly there was a flash of light, and the storm calmed. King Triton had arrived at the lagoon.

"What has happened here?" King Triton roared.

Eric looked down humbly. "It is entirely my fault, Sir," he explained. "I built this wall to make a nice place for Ariel to visit her friends. I was wrong."

The king of the seas glared at Eric. Then with a hint of a smile, he added, "Well, you are human, after all."

With a wave of his trident, King Triton called to all the dolphins and they quickly found the baby dolphin's mother! Frantically, she tried to get into the lagoon.

"Oh, dear!" Ariel exclaimed. "The gate won't open! She can't get in!"

Eric looked at King Triton. "Do you mind?"

"Not at all," the king replied. "Swim back, everyone!" He raised his trident and blasted down the wall.

There was no royal ball that night at the palace. Instead, Eric and Ariel returned to the lagoon and danced under the sparkling stars.

"I love this place," Ariel said to her husband. "Thank you."

Just then the baby dolphin and his mother entered the lagoon, surfaced and playfully splashed the prince and princess.

"I think that means we are forgiven!" Ariel laughed.

The End

Aurora and the Helpful Dragon

By Barbara Bazaldua

Illustrated by Studio IBOIX and Gabriella Matta

I'll race you to the lookout point!" Princess Aurora called to Prince Phillip as they galloped through the forest one sunny fall morning. She sped away on her horse, Moonlight, with Prince Phillip close behind.

Just as Aurora and Phillip rounded a bend, they heard a funny noise. A small dragon popped from behind a tree and scampered toward Aurora.

"Oh, he's so cute!" Aurora exclaimed as she dismounted.

"Grrgrrgrr?" the little dragon murmured, clambering into Aurora's lap.

But Phillip wanted to protect his wife. "Dragons can be dangerous!"

The little dragon shook his head, no.

"I think he's saying he's not dangerous," Aurora laughed. "Please, let's take him home. I'm going to name him Crackle!"

"He does seem like a harmless little fellow," Phillip agreed. But Moonlight was still afraid. She tossed her mane and pawed the ground. Crackle's tail drooped sadly. Then he grinned his funny little grin. Suddenly, he licked Moonlight's nose with his long, warm tongue. Moonlight blinked with surprise and nuzzled Crackle under the chin. The little dragon giggled.

"Moonlight likes Crackle!" Aurora laughed.

When Phillip and Aurora rode into the courtyard, the three fairies were
hanging banners for King Stefan and the Queen who were coming for a ball
that night.

"Come, my dear, let's practise dancing!" Phillip said to his princess.

But Flora gasped when she saw Crackle. "Dragons can be dangerous."

"Remember the last one!" Fauna added.

"Oooh, I think he's sweet," Merryweather spoke up.

"Grrrgrr," Crackle babbled.

"He thinks you're sweet, too," Aurora told Merryweather as Prince Phillip
swept his princess across the courtyard. Just then, Crackle noticed a kitten in
Fauna's workbasket.

113

Crackle listened to the cute kitten purring. Crackle scrunched up his mouth and closed his eyes.

"Purrgrr, purrgrr!" Crackle tried to purr. Clouds of smoke puffed from his nose and mouth.

"Aachoo! Aachooooie! Ah-ah-ah-CHOO!" The fairies sneezed so hard that they fluttered backwards.

"Please – achoo – stop trying to purr!" Fauna exclaimed.

Crackle looked sad for a moment. Then he saw the kitten playing with a ball of yarn from the workbasket, and his eyes lit up. He snatched a ball of yarn with his mouth. *Whoosh!* – it caught fire. Merryweather put the fire out with her wand.

"Oh, Crackle," Aurora said gently. "You're not a kitten. You're a dragon."

Crackle's lower lip trembled.

Just then, Crackle saw Phillip leading the horses into the stables. A dog followed Phillip barking and wagging it's tail. Crackle wagged his tail and ran to the stables, too.

"Woofgrr, woofgrr," he tried to bark. Flames shot from his mouth and caught some straw on fire. Phillip poured water on the burning straw.

"You're not a dog," he said kindly, shooing Crackle away.

When Aurora saw Crackle creep from the stable, she carried him into the castle and cuddled him on a window seat. A bird was singing outside. Crackle's ears perked up and his eyes shone hopefully.

"LAAAlaagrr!" he bellowed.

King Hubert heard the racket and rushed into the room. "Oh, my, my, my! How did a dragon get in here?" he blustered.

Frightened by the king, Crackle jumped from the window seat and ran into the garden. Aurora ran after him. At last she found the little dragon sitting beside a waterfall that splashed down from one pool to another. Crackle was studying a fish swimming in the lowest pool.

Before Aurora could stop him, Crackle splashed into the water. The startled fish leaped into a higher pool.

"Crackle, you're not a fish!" Aurora exclaimed as she pulled Crackle from the pool. "You're not a kitten, or a dog, or a bird either. You're a dragon!"

Tears rolled down Crackle's face. "Grrgrrgrr," he sobbed.

Suddenly, Aurora understood. "Do you think no one will like you because you're a dragon?" she asked. Crackle nodded and whimpered sadly.

"Crackle, you can't change being a dragon," Aurora said kindly. "But you don't have to be a dangerous dragon. You can be a brave, helpful dragon."

Crackle stopped crying. "Grrgrrgrrgrr?" he growled hopefully. Before Aurora could answer, thunder boomed. Wind blew black clouds over the sun. Aurora snatched up Crackle. She reached the castle doors just as the rain began to pour down.

Everyone was gathered in the grand hallway, watching the storm.

"I'm afraid King Stefan and the Queen might lose their way on the road above the cliffs," Prince Phillip said, his voice filled with concern. "I should ride out to help."

Aurora looked at Crackle. "Do you want to show everyone that you're a brave and helpful dragon?" she asked.

"GRRRgrrrgrr!" Crackle exclaimed enthusiastically.

123

"Fly to the top of the highest castle tower," Aurora explained. "Then blow the largest, brightest flames you can."

Aurora watched him as the little fellow soared upward.

"Come on, everyone!" the princess called. She ran to get a better view of the watch tower, with Phillip and the others following closely behind.

Everyone tried to see Crackle at the top of the tower, but the storm was too dark and strong. Suddenly, they saw huge flames, and they were coming from little Crackle! Gold and red light flashed up into the sky above the watch tower.

Again and again, Crackle blew his flames until, at last, Phillip shouted. "I see King Stefan and the Queen! They're almost here!"

Everyone hurried to greet the visiting royals.

"The tower light saved us!" King Stefan exclaimed. "I need one like it!"

At that moment Crackle flew happily to join in the fun.

"Well, there he is! Our new tower light," King Hubert said with a laugh.

"A dragon?" King Stefan asked. "But dragons are danger—"

"Not Crackle," Aurora interrupted. "He's a brave and helpful dragon!"

That night at the ball, Crackle lit the candles, warmed food and kept the fireplace blazing. King Hubert and the fairies were so pleased that they took turns scratching Crackle beneath his chin.

As Prince Phillip and Aurora danced, Crackle trotted beside them. Outside, it was cold and stormy. But inside, everyone was happy and warm – especially Crackle the helpful dragon.

The End

Rapunzel's Story

Adapted by Lisa Marsoli
Illustrated by Jean-Paul Orpinas, Studio IBOIX,
and the Disney Storybook Artists

Once upon a time, in a land far away, a drop of sunlight fell to the ground. It grew into a magical golden flower that possessed healing powers. An old woman named Mother Gothel discovered the flower, and hoarded its power to preserve her youth and beauty.

As centuries passed, a glorious kingdom was built close to the cliff where the flower grew. When the beloved queen fell ill, the townspeople found the legendary flower. The flower made the Queen well, and she soon gave birth to a beautiful baby girl.

The King and Queen launched a lantern into the sky in celebration.

One night, the vengeful Mother Gothel slipped into the nursery, where she discovered that the healing power of the flower had transferred into the baby's golden hair!

Mother Gothel knew that if she wanted to stay young, she had to keep the child with her always. She snatched the princess and vanished to a place where no one could find them. The King and Queen were heartbroken.

Each year on the princess's birthday, the King and Queen released lanterns into the night sky. They hoped their light would guide their princess home.

Mother Gothel kept Rapunzel locked in a soaring tower and raised her as a daughter. She only truly loved Rapunzel's golden hair.

Rapunzel was happy with the companionship of Mother Gothel and her friend Pascal, the chameleon. But on the day before her eighteenth birthday, Rapunzel told Mother Gothel she had one dream. "I want to see the floating lights!" she said, revealing a painting she had made of them. "They appear every year on my birthday – only on my birthday. And I can't help but feel like they're meant for me!"

Mother Gothel told Rapunzel she was too helpless to handle the outside world.

134

Meanwhile, in another part of the forest, a thief named Flynn Rider was on the run with his partners in crime, the Stabbington brothers. Flynn clutched tightly to a satchel that held a stolen royal crown!

Flynn knew the Stabbingtons were too dangerous to be trusted, so he left them and took off with the satchel. But the Captain of the Guard and his horse Maximus were on his heels! The tricky thief knocked the Captain off Maximus and landed in the saddle himself. Maximus spun in circles until he sunk his teeth into the satchel. As Flynn yanked the satchel free, it went flying into the air.

The satchel snagged on a tree that extended over a cliff. Flynn and Maximus both made their way out onto the tree trunk. But the tree broke, sending the thief and horse toppling into the canyon below.

When they landed, Flynn took off before Maximus could pick up his scent. The thief ducked into a cave. When he emerged from the other side, he saw something amazing: an enormous tower. It would make the perfect hiding place!

He climbed the tower and scrambled into the open window at the top. Finally, he breathed a sigh of relief. He was safe!

CLANG! Suddenly, everything went black.

Rapunzel had been so startled, she hit him with a frying pan! Flynn was the first man she had ever seen. He didn't look like the scary ruffians that Mother Gothel had warned her about. Rapunzel thought he was actually pleasant-looking.

After making sure he was unconscious, Rapunzel stuffed him inside the wardrobe. She felt exhilarated! Surely this act of bravery would prove to Mother that she could handle herself in the outside world.

Then Rapunzel noticed the mysterious gold object in Flynn's satchel. She placed it on top of her head and gazed into the mirror. She felt different somehow.

Suddenly, Mother Gothel arrived. Rapunzel brought up the floating lights again.

"We're done talking about this. You are not leaving this tower! EVER!" roared Mother Gothel.

Ever? Rapunzel was shocked. Realizing she would never get out of the tower unless she took matters into her own hands, Rapunzel asked for another birthday present. She requested special paint that would require Mother Gothal to leave on a three-day journey.

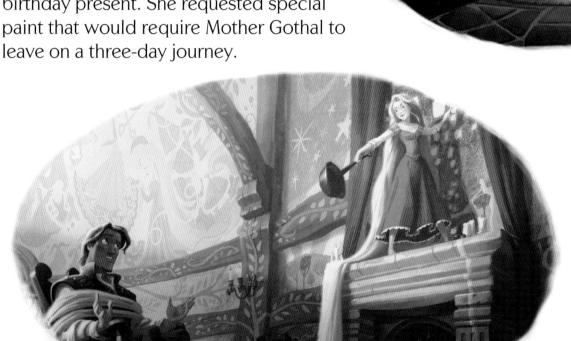

Mother Gothel agreed to get the paint and left the tower. Not wasting another second, Rapunzel dragged Flynn out of the closet and offered him a deal. If Flynn took her to see the floating lights and returned her home safely, she would give him the satchel. Flynn had no choice but to agree.

As much as Rapunzel longed to leave the tower, when the moment came, she was terrified. She had never been outside before. But when she glanced back at her painting of the floating lights, Rapunzel overcame her fear and leaped!

With Pascal on her shoulder, she slid down her hair, stopping just inches above the ground. Slowly, Rapunzel touched one foot to the soft grass, then the other.

"I can't believe I did this! I can't believe I did this! I can't believe I did this!" she shouted as she rolled on the ground.

Rapunzel was having the time of her life, but she also felt like a terrible daughter for betraying Mother Gothel. One moment she was running gleefully through a meadow, the next she was sobbing facedown in a field of flowers.

Flynn tried to take advantage of Rapunzel's guilt by making her feel even worse. "Does your mother deserve this?" he asked. "No. Would it break her heart? Of course. I'm letting you out of the deal. Let's turn around and get you home."

Flynn's charms didn't work on Rapunzel. "I'm seeing those lanterns," she insisted.

Not far from the tower, Mother Gothel came face to face with Maximus. "A palace horse," she gasped, seeing the kingdom's sun symbol on Maximus' chest. She thought the guards had found Rapunzel. She turned and frantically raced back to the tower.

Mother Gothel searched everywhere, but Rapunzel was gone. Then she saw something shiny beneath the staircase. It was the crown in the satchel, along with Flynn's WANTED poster. Now she knew exactly who had taken Rapunzel – and nothing was going to stop her from finding him!

By this time, Flynn had led Rapunzel to a cosy-looking pub called the Snuggly Duckling. But inside, the place was filled with scary-looking thugs! Flynn was hoping to frighten Rapunzel into returning to the tower.

Then someone held up Flynn's WANTED poster. The pub thugs began fighting for the reward money – with Flynn caught right in the middle of the brawl.

Rapunzel banged her frying pan on a giant pot to get the thugs' attention. She asked them to let Flynn go so that she could make her dream come true. To Rapunzel's surprise, every one of the thugs had a secret dream, too.

Outside, Mother Gothel arrived at the pub. She looked into the window, and was shocked to see that Rapunzel had managed to befriend a room full of ruffians!

Suddenly, Maximus, the royal guards and the captive Stabbington brothers burst into the pub. "Where's Rider?" demanded the Captain.

One of the thugs revealed a secret passageway to Flynn and Rapunzel. They gratefully disappeared into the dark tunnel.

Moments later, Maximus led the guards straight to the escape route. After they had left, the Stabbington brothers broke free and headed down the passageway themselves. They wanted the crown back!

Mother Gothel had seen everything, and made one of the thugs tell her where the tunnel ended.

Flynn and Rapunzel sprinted through the tunnel and skidded to the edge of an enormous cavern. They managed to swing across the wide chasm using Rapunzel's hair.

But they weren't safe yet. A dam suddenly burst, filling the entire cavern with water! Maximus, the guards and the Stabbingtons were washed away, and Flynn and Rapunzel were trapped in a small cave. The water quickly began to rise.

"This is all my fault," Rapunzel said tearfully. "I'm so sorry, Flynn."

"Eugene. My real name's Eugene Fitzherbert," Flynn admitted. "Someone might as well know."

Rapunzel revealed a secret of her own: "I have magic hair that glows when I sing." Then, she suddenly realized her hair could light up the cave and show them the way out!

At the tunnel's exit, Mother Gothel waited for Flynn and Rapunzel, but the Stabbington brothers emerged instead. She offered them revenge on Flynn – and something even more valuable than the crown. The Stabbington brothers liked the sound of that!

Meanwhile, Rapunzel, Flynn and Pascal had made it safely to shore. Rapunzel wrapped her hair around Flynn's injured hand and began to sing. Her glowing hair healed Flynn's wound. Flynn was dumbfounded. He was finally beginning to understand how truly special Rapunzel was.

146

When Flynn went off to gather firewood, Mother Gothel appeared from the shadows. She handed Rapunzel the satchel with the crown and told her that it was all Flynn wanted. Once Rapunzel gave it to him, the thief would vanish. Mother Gothel set these seeds of doubt, then retreated back into the forest. Rapunzel wanted to trust Flynn but she wasn't sure. She decided to hide the satchel.

The next morning, Flynn woke up to Maximus trying to drag him away! Rapunzel came to Flynn's rescue and talked the horse into letting the thief go free for one more day. As Flynn and Maximus shook on their truce, a bell rang in the distance. Rapunzel ran towards it until she came to the crest of a hill.

Rapunzel gasped as the entire kingdom came into view. Her dream was just hours away from coming true!

Rapunzel, Flynn, Maximus and Pascal entered the gates of the kingdom. The town was the most exciting thing Rapunzel had ever experienced. A little boy greeted Rapunzel with a kingdom flag that had a golden sun symbol on it. Then a group of little girls braided Rapunzel's locks and pinned them up with flowers.

Afterwards, Rapunzel and Flynn joined a crowd as a dance was about to begin.

Rapunzel was transfixed by a mosaic behind the stage. It was of the King and Queen holding a baby girl with striking green eyes, just like her own.

"Let the dance begin!" called an announcer.

Rapunzel and Flynn joined hands and began to whirl around the square.

After they danced, the couple visited shops and enjoyed the sights. All the while, they were getting to know each other better. It was a wonderful day!

As evening approached, Flynn led Rapunzel to a boat and rowed them to a spot with a perfect view of the kingdom. As lanterns filled the sky, Rapunzel's heart soared. She gave Flynn the satchel, which she had kept hidden all day. She was no longer afraid he would leave her once he had the crown.

Beneath the glow of the lanterns, Rapunzel and Flynn held hands and gazed into each other's eyes.

But their romantic moment ended abruptly when Flynn spotted the Stabbington brothers watching them from the shore. Quickly, he rowed the boat to land.

"I'll be right back," he told Rapunzel as he grabbed the satchel and strode off. Flynn gave the brothers the crown, but they wanted Rapunzel and her magic hair instead! He turned to go to Rapunzel, but the brothers knocked him unconscious, tied him to the helm of a boat and set him sailing into the harbour.

Then they came for Rapunzel. The brothers told her that Flynn had traded her for the crown. Rapunzel saw Flynn sailing away. She thought he had betrayed her!

Rapunzel ran off into the forest with the brothers in pursuit. Moments later, she heard Mother Gothel's voice. She ran back and found Mother standing over the unconscious Stabbingtons.

"You were right, Mother," said Rapunzel tearfully, hugging her tight.

Flynn's boat eventually crashed into a dock. Two guards found him tied up with the stolen crown and immediately dragged him off to prison. Maximus witnessed everything and knew he had to do something to save both Flynn and Rapunzel.

As Flynn was led down the prison corridors by the guards, he spotted the Stabbington brothers in a nearby cell. They admitted that Mother Gothel had told them about Rapunzel's hair and double-crossed them.

Suddenly, the pub thugs from the Snuggly Duckling arrived and broke Flynn out of jail! They launched him over the prison walls and onto Maximus' back. Maximus had planned the entire escape! Flynn thanked him and, together, the heroes galloped off to rescue Rapunzel.

Back at the tower, a heartbroken Rapunzel held up the kingdom flag with the sun symbol and gazed at her wall of art. Then she noticed something amazing – she had been painting the sun symbol her whole life. She suddenly realized that she was the lost princess! But before Rapunzel could reach the window to escape, Mother Gothel overpowered her.

Flynn finally arrived. "Rapunzel! Rapunzel, let down your hair!" he called. When he reached the top, he found Rapunzel chained in the middle of the room. He went to help her, but Mother Gothel wounded him with a dagger.

Rapunzel begged Mother Gothel to allow her to heal Flynn. In return, Rapunzel promised Mother Gothel she would stay with her forever.

Mother Gothel knew Rapunzel never broke a promise. She agreed to the deal and unchained Rapunzel.

Rapunzel rushed to Flynn's side and placed her hair over his wound. "No, Rapunzel, don't do this," begged Flynn.

"I'll be fine," said Rapunzel, looking into Flynn's eyes. "If you're okay, I'll be fine."

Flynn caressed her cheek. Then he suddenly reached for a shard of broken glass and cut off her hair! It instantly turned brown and lost its magic healing power.

"What have you done?!" Mother Gothel cried. Within moments she aged hundreds of years and turned to dust.

Rapunzel cradled Flynn in her arms and began to weep. A single golden tear fell upon Flynn's cheek. To Rapunzel's astonishment, the tear – and then Flynn's entire body – began to glow.

Flynn was healed. "Rapunzel!" he exclaimed.

The two embraced and shared their first kiss.

Flynn, Pascal and Maximus brought Rapunzel straight to the castle. Her parents rushed to hug her. They were filled with joy. Their daughter had finally been returned to them! Rapunzel felt her parents' love surround her as they all hugged each other tightly, a family once more.

Soon, all of the townspeople gathered for a welcome home party. The King and Queen were there, along with Flynn, Pascal, Maximus and the pub thugs. The people of the kingdom released floating lanterns into the sky. Their light had guided their princess home at last.

The End